Anonymous

Legends and Poetry of the Hudson

Anonymous

Legends and Poetry of the Hudson

ISBN/EAN: 9783337155698

Printed in Europe, USA, Canada, Australia, Japan

Cover: Foto ©Andreas Hilbeck / pixelio.de

More available books at **www.hansebooks.com**

LEGENDS AND POETRY

OF THE

HUDSON.

NEW YORK:

P. S. WYNKOOP & SON, 108 FULTON STREET.

1868.

SYNOPSIS.

LEGENDS AND POETRY OF THE HUDSON.

Search made by the Indian tribes for a fountain of "Fire Water," which, soon after the arrival of the Settlers, they believed to be the cause of the crooked and winding course of the River—Many of the Legends almost buried in the ashes of our Fathers' Firesides.

THE SHATE-MUC.

The Graves of our Heroes, Poets and Statesmen under the clear sky by the side of bright waters—No place in our Country where Poetry and Romance are so blended with the Heroic of our History as along the banks of the Hudson.

INDIAN LEGENDS AND TRADITIONS.

The Death and Prophecy of the Great King of the Mohegans at Castleberg—The Ship of Hendrich Hudson, "The Half Moon."—The Storehouse of Legends and Traditions—The Catskills—The Squaw Spirit of the Mountains—The last Indian Battle upon the River.

DUTCH LEGENDS AND HISTORY.

The first Dutch Settlers—Wouter Van Twiller—Their Hearth-stones and Hospitable Firesides—The Ruins of an old Mansion on an Island in a Lake in the County of Columbia—A strange Poem, found here above an old mantle signed "Annie K. Dote," entitled " The Revolutionary Captain who took the District School "—The Storm Ship, whose crew afterward entertained Rip Van Winkle— "The Legend of Dobbs' Ferry," a Poem—The Customs and Habits of our Mothers, as well as our Fathers—The old Dutch Churches.

REVOLUTIONARY SKETCHES.

The First Messenger along the old Post Road proclaiming War—The Battle Grounds of Saratoga, Stillwater, Old

THE LEGENDS AND POETRY OF

THE HUDSON.

I T was for a long time a traditional belief among the Indian tribes which dwelt along the banks of the Hudson, that the water, ages ago, broke through the opposing barrier of the Highlands, draining a great lake and forming the channel of the river. How they became possessed of an idea so much in accordance with the results of science, or where they obtained many other traditional notions quite consistent with the progress of humanity, will probably ever be shrouded in a mystery as difficult to unravel as an attempt to trace the genealogy of the Incas to the time when Ararat's cradle rocked the infant world. But soon after the arrival of our worthy ancestors, and their quiet settlement at Communipaw, a species of *Jug*-glery—a sort of modern " traveling companion " to civilization — tended to confuse somewhat the minds of the natives, disturbing many of their original beliefs, and particularly this traditional idea concerning the *winding channel* of the Shate-muc. Whether this refinement of European *extraction*—so universally appreciated by the aborigines — was introduced to simplify the art of making bargains in respect to the purchase of furs and the acquisition of territory ; or whether its ameliorating effect on a race unused to much

gaiety of temper and flow of spirits only
afforded an innocent amusement to our philo-
sophical progenitors, and suggested the original
plan of those irregular zigzag fences which still
stand in our valleys and along our hill-sides, the
muse of history and the pinions of tradition
have failed to record. It came, however, in
some way, to be generally believed by the Red
men, that the crooked and winding channel of
the river was not wholly attributable to its
own inclination; but, deep in the Northern
forests, near some favorite haunt of the "Great
Spirit," a fountain of what they termed "Fire
Water," always clear and sparkling, bubbled
from the ground, and the river, drinking of
this water as it flowed into its bosom, naturally
found a wandering way to the sea. In accordance with this theory, they rejected their
former idea that the Highlands had ever been
sundered, and chose rather to believe that the

mountains and little hills, impelled by curiosity, had come from the East and the West to see this strange phenomenon, and either attracted by each other's beauty, or loving the music of the water, had willingly remained upon its banks. To find this wonderful fountain, the warriors were willing to encounter any perils and endure any hardships. Every little lake in the North Woods which found an outlet in the river was visited with a zeal and eagerness which gives the blush to modern explorers; every trickling rivulet was tasted, but the clear cold water only laughed merrily in their faces and sweetly kissed their parched lips as they stooped to drink of its purity. Up the tributary streams, far into the land of the Mohawks, almost to the hunting grounds of the Oneidas; up the rapid Sacandaga to beautiful "Lake . Pleasant," mirroring in its sleeping waters the same pines and hemlocks as two hundred years

ago ; along the bright-flowing Hoosick, beyond
the "Strange Chimney" of doubtful utility,
and the ever green "Council Square" where
the tribes were wont to assemble in the realm
of the Schacokes ; up the Battenkill to the
clear fountain which murmurs a response to
the gentle flowing of Otter Creek, on its way
to the blue waters of Champlain ; up the
Poestenkill, honored in later years by an im-
probable legend ; up the Kinderhook and
Claverack Creeks, frequently referred to in
rythmic measure by the fair daughters of
Columbia ; far away to the Taghconic range,
whose Eastern slope loses its waters in the
deep ravines of the old Stockbridge Chiefs, and
the beautiful hills where the Green River and
Jansen's Creek, born of twin fountains, bid
each other an early adieu ; the former seeking
the valley of the Housatonic, while the latter,
joyful with the music of Bash-Bish, brings to

the Eastern bank of the river a heart full of
traditional beauty. But in vain! The Helder-
berg Hills and the lordly Catskills gave no
token of this strange fountain, more wonderful
than those fountains of Love and Hatred near
the fabled palace of Alcina. The warriors only
returned to speak of the crystal lakes and
little brooklets, whose sources, deeply buried
in the Northern forests for long years, will
never know the sunshine.

And although the fabled fountain is still
undiscovered, yet these early and diligent
explorers learned much of other tribes and
customs, and had many stories to relate of the
fairy lands they visited. So every person who
wanders along the banks of our river, whether
in search of its legendary history or strolling
without a purpose amid its monuments and its
beauty, must necessarily gather many beautiful
stories from lips which will soon be silent, some

local in their nature, and others of general
interest ; more than this, beautiful sketches, to
be completed in dreams and colored in sweet
hours of reverie, are stamped for ever upon the
recollection to make cheerful the "gallery of
memory," where we all are hanging some new
picture day by day. Bright among these
pictures, as we look back through the elm-
shaded vista of four years, are the Summer
strolls along the banks of the Hudson, and the
fairy castles, with turret, dome and battlement,
which the setting sun often builds upon the
Catskills, are full of reality to some of our
readers, although the foundations are not laid
in mortar and the superstructures are only
sunbeams. In these wanderings we have found
a few strange stories and legends almost lost
and forgotten in that most sad of burial
places — the ashes of our father's fire-sides.
And although others may have already obtained

the "Golden Fleece," and given to the world a master history of their voyages and adventures, there still remain beautiful legends to be narrated concerning this land of Colchis. To collect a few of these legends and some of the poetical incidents of the history of our river, in the form of an essay, was undertaken at the request of friends, and read in some of the towns and cities along its banks. The old Indian traditions, the Dutch legends, the Revolutionary sketches, and the beauty of its scenery, were crowded into a few pages of manuscript that the patience of kind hearers might not be wearied. We have been asked to print it exactly as delivered, without changing a word or sentence, and, save the insertion of a *quaint poem*—the original manuscript of which lately fell into our possession, entitled, "The Revolutionary Captain who took the District School"—we present it *verbatim, literatim, punctuatim.* And whether an hour is passed pleasantly or otherwise in perusing " The Legends and poetry of the Shate-muc," it is at least gratifying to the writer, and all who love our beautiful Hudson, that the River will ever flow on just as tranquilly to the sea, and the little brooks which supply it will continue to sing as musically and flow as gently as ever did " Sweet Afton " along our own happy cottages where live the True, the Good and the Beautiful.

THE SHATE-MUC.

IN a lecture recently delivered by a late member of the English Parliament, in some of the towns along the banks of our River, there was the following sentence: "When I am visited by my friends from America and show them the river Thames, they turn away laughing and say, 'Why there are *ditches* full of water running through our farms larger than that;' but when I take them to Westminster Abbey and show them the burial places of our Kings, our Philosophers and our Poets, the glorious memories which cluster about that solemn place fill them with wonder and astonishment." Perhaps he did not intend in this sentence to speak lightly of the American People or their history : but if it was the expression of that overbearing spirit which some are inclined to consider *natural* to the English People, and it was only a polite way of saying, " You Americans have indeed splendid scenery, cloud-capped mountains and majestic rivers : but where are the graves of your Heroes, your Poets and your Statesmen," we would answer, " It is true we have not a history reaching back through thirteen centuries, lost in the dim twilight of fable ; we have no monumental ruins covered with the ivy of ages almost unknown: and yet along the beautiful banks of our streams and rivers stand monuments which need no *antiquity* to give them glory, or bolts and bars to preserve them from the hand of sacrilege." England can well be proud of the names carved on her marble sepulchres (and we share the glory with her), but when she asks, "Where are the graves of your Heroes, your Statesmen, your Poets, and your Martyrs in the sacred cause of liberty," we point to Mount Vernon, to the quiet shades of Ashland, to the green groves of Monticello, to the grave of a martyred President, to the plain slab at Sunnyside, to the tombless dead of Saratoga, and more than all, if she asks for the graves of Heroes, we point to the Southern battle-fields, to the mounds of those who perished in Southern dungeons, over whose unknown graves fair flowers spring up as if conscious of those who sleep beneath, and upon which the nightly stars look down, crystal lights in the blue dome of nature's temple, compared with which the arches of Westminster Abbey are unworthy of a thought!

"On fame's eternal camping ground
    Their snow-white tents are spread,
And glory guards with solemn round
    The bivouacs of the dead."

We have no national Thesaurus of our illustrious departed, no aristocratic arcade of whited sepulchres or arched avenues of "dull, cold marble," where royal magnificence and worthy genius are separated from their dearest friends, and live, even in their burial, an eternal exile from the green graves of those they loved. But we turn with pride as a people from the "gathering place" of England's glory to the mountains, streams and rivers of our own country, where the echo of heroic deeds still lingers.

Here are the burial-places of our Heroes, Poets and Statesmen, under the clear sky, by the side of bright waters, sleeping in the very spots their memory and deeds have

hallowed ; and as our first martyrs and Statesmen, by the noble struggle of their lives,
achieved here a *Truth* which is stranger than
fiction — the successful revolution of three
millions of people against the most powerful
nationality in the world, and *thus* blended with
the early poetry and romance of these hills and
valleys an inspiration born of patriotism, it
is fitting that their graves should be scattered,
as we find them, among the mounds of a
strange people who once possessed these broad
hunting grounds.

And there is no other place in our country
where this poetry and romance are so strangely
blended with the heroic of our history as along
the banks of our Hudson. No other river
where the waves of different civilizations have
left so many *waifs* upon the banks ; no valley
where the fireside-tale is more poetical, where
even the streams and townships, by the very

names they bear, perpetuate our early history ;
and we trust that all who love our river,
and sometimes *sigh* in the beautiful lines of
Whittier—

" That our broad lands—our sea-like lakes,
And mountains piled to the clouds— *   *   *
*   *   * Our valleys, lovelier than those
Which the old poets sung of—*should but figure*
On the apocryphal chart of speculation,
As pastures, wood lots, mill-sites with the
    privileges,
Rights and appurtenances, which make up
A *Yankee Paradise.* Even their names,
Whose melody yet lingers like the last
Vibration of the Red Man's requiem,
Exchanged for syllables significant
Of cotton-mill and rail-car, will look kindly
Upon this effort to call up the ghost
Of our dim past, and listen with pleased ear
To the responses of the questioned shade."

Four hundred years are not yet completed
since the " Te Deum Laudamus " burst from
grateful hearts as the first footsteps of a

civilized people pressed the shores of a new world. Four brief centuries, hardly space sufficient for the *nap* of Italy, wearied with the struggles of two thousand years, have worked in our own country a change more marvelous than a dream, revealing in quick panoramic succession, the various phases from the wildest tradition to the most stirring history, from the lowest barbarism to a refined civilization. This first song of a Christian people upon our shores, " We praise thee, O God," was the fitting *dedecation* of a country where free institutions were to find an enduring home, and every year takes up the words of Columbus and his bold followers, "Te Deum Laudamus!"

Back to the old country were carried strange stories of the people dwelling upon these wild and uncultivated shores. The Philosopher and Alchemist again dreamed of the fountains of eternal youth—the elixir of life. The Poet saw 'n imagination the Arcadia of the West, hung with the apples of Iduna and the Avaricious saw a land of gold and silver !

Nor were the tales told by the Indian council-fires less strange and marvelous, every year taking new form where tradition was the only history. "How the pale face come from the land of the sun, borne by a great bird across the big waters," and many a chief seemed to see, as it were in prophetic vision, the westward march of his people. And it is related of the great chief of the Mohegans, the king of the tribes which dwelt along the "king of rivers," (for so they called our Hudson) as his spirit was passing away to the hunting grounds of the Great Manito, that he pointed southward and said, "I see the traditions of my fathers are true. I see *far, far* away the 'big bird' again floating upon the waters, so far my warriors that *you* can not see it, but ere two

Autumns have scattered the leaves upon my grave, the pale face will claim our hunting grounds."

And when the ship of Hendrick Hudson, appropriately christened " The Half Moon," —its bow and stern rising high above the centre of the deck,—floated about as leisurely as its god-mother in the ethereal blue along the little villages of cedar wigwams, the warriors remembered with sadness the last words of their chief. And it may still be in the memory of some living that one of this tribe, bowed with age, returned to look for the last time upon the river of his fathers ; and as he stood *alone* upon the hills of the Shate-muc, and saw the changes of three quarters of a century, in his silent submission we can well imagine he felt even more than the sad lines of the Poet :

"O ! stream of the mountains, if answer of
    thine
Could rise from thy waters to questions of mine,
Methinks, through the din of the thronged
    banks, a moan
Of sorrow would swell for the days that are
    gone."

Many years ago the prophecy of the old
chief was more than fulfilled, and nothing now
remains of many of the river tribes, save here
and there the mound of some warrior and
strange legends or traditions. Perhaps none
so strange or romantic as "The Lover's Leap,"
on the banks of the Housatonic, where an
Indian maiden is said to have jumped from a
cliff two hundred feet high, with a blue cotton
umbrella, and escaped unharmed. But where
she obtained the umbrella in her flight, or how
from this strangely poetical circumstance, the
cliff was ever called "The Lover's Leap," no
ne is able to tell. Or, perhaps we have no

legend so beautifully narrated as thy story of
" Monument Mountain," by Bryant, wherein a
beautiful Indian girl is represented as dying *all
for love*. But the real legend, when partially
disrobed of its poetic garb, is simply that about
seventy years ago, an Indian woman,

> Whose hair "was gray,
> And gray with years "

Hated by the whole community, was induced to
leap from the cliff for a quart of rum, and the
true version of the story can be seen upon the
five dollar bills of the old Maihaiwe Bank.
We have no legends exactly like these, nor
does the dark cruelty of a " Wyoming Mas-
sacre" stain our banks. But the great *storehouse* of legends and traditions, which no other
river possesses are the Catskills, which, about
midway between the ocean and the crystal
fountains of the North, stand like sentinels of
the valley. They were called by the Indians

the Onti-o-ra's, or Mountains of the sky, as they sometimes seem like clouds along the horizon. This range of mountains was supposed by the Indians to have been originally a monster who devoured all the children of the Red Men, and that the Great Spirit touched him when he was going down to the salt lake to bathe, and here he remains. " Two little lakes upon the summit were regarded the eyes of the monster, and these are open all the summer ; but in the winter they are covered with a thick crust or heavy film ; but whether sleeping or waking tears always trickle down his cheeks. In these mountains, according to Indian belief, was kept the great treasury of storm and sunshine, presided over by an old squaw spirit who dwelt on the highest peak of the mountains. She kept day and night shut up in her wigwam, letting out only one at a time. She manufactured new moons every

month, cutting up the old ones into stars," and,
like the old Æolus of mythology, shut the winds
up in the caverns of the hills.

There is also a traditional account that the
last Indian battle fought upon our river was
between the Mohawks and the Mohegans, and,
as the old king of the Mohegans was dying after
the conflict was over, he commanded his regalia
to be taken off and his son put into the king-
ship while his eyes were yet clear to behold
him.   Over forty years had he worn it from the
time he received it in London from Queen Anne,
on all festive occasions, whether of war or peace.
He asked his son to kneel at his couch, and,
putting his withered hand across his brow,
placed the feathery crown upon his head and
gave the silver-mounted tomahawk, symbols of
power to rule and power to execute.   Then,
looking up to the heavens, he said, as if in de-
spair for his race: "The hills are our pillows

and the broad plains to the west our hunting
grounds, our brothers are called into the bright
wigwam of the Everlasting, and our bones lie
upon the fields of many battles, but the wisdom of the dead is given to the living."

On the same evening, just as the sun was
bidding the world "good night," and the shadows, creeping from their hiding-places, deepened the hue of the distant Catskills where the
setting sun was again closing it's daily volume
of untarnished blue and gold, they laid the
chief in his last bed, at the foot of the
hill not far from Castleberg. Any one, it is
said, will tell you, if you venture there, where
the Indian graves are made; and, in the language of the writer who has chronicled this
battle, " From that Castleberg his grave is seen
with this mountain stream placidly winding
around it, and the great river over which he
reigned so long still winds on with majestic

flow; and as we have stood on that rising
ground at sunset, looking to the mountains on
which there lay palaces, castles, islands, and
smooth blue lakes of spiritual beauty, we have,
at times, almost envied the men who imagined
these near glories to be the grounds and the
streams to which the last king of the rivers departed "—for his son never ruled a day.

These are some of our early legends and we
ought not willingly let them die, for they have
more of poetry and more of truth than the old
struggles of Gods and Heroes; the wars of the
Cid, or the adventures of Launcelot and the
Knights of the Round Table. Under the green
forest spires of "God's first temples" these warriors of the forest continually worshiped the
incarnation of the Great Spirit, seeing the hand
of the Manito in all creation. They knew no
idols! for, in the simplicity of their lives, they
lived so near to nature that they heard the beat-

ing of her heart, and in "the bright wigwam of the Everlasting,' far to the southwest, they believed a deity resided who cared for his children, and continually they feared and adored him.

> " And is not nature's worship thus—
>   Ceaseless, ever going on;
> Hath It not a voice for us
>   In the thunder or the tone
> Of the leaf-harp, faint and small,
>   Speaking to the *unsealed* ear,
>   Words of blended love and fear
> Of the mighty soul of all."

Closely blended with these Indian traditions we have the early tales and legends of the first Dutch settlers along the rich valley of the Hudson and its tributary streams. Living peaceably with the world, and having no ambition reaching beyond the welfare of their friends and neighbors, with no pleasures beyond their own quiet firesides, a proverbial hospitality was

developed, and the early history of the Hudson
gives us a picture of contentment, of pure hap-
piness and rural simplicity, which no other section of our country has ever been able to present. They did not bring with them, perhaps,
from the fatherland the enthusiasm of those
who, escaping from the tyranny of England,
felt the glow and impulse of Liberty, as it was,
rising from the grave of bigotry, but they
brought that *persistency* which, in years before,
had diked Holland from the ocean and made the
marshes of the old Batavii a hailing-place
among the nations—a persistency which was
destined to make the little valley of the Hudson the richest in our country, and at its portal
place the Emporium of the Continent. They
may have been less interested in discussing the
prated rights of man, but we imagine they en-
joyed themselves quite as well as the inhabitants of witch-haunted Boston in the long days

of Puritan fanaticism. They were not an impulsive people, and yet the citizens of New York city passed the first resolutions to import nothing from the Mother Country, burned ten boxes of stamps sent from England before any other colony or city had made even a show of resistance, and, when the Declaration was read, pulled down the leaden statue of George III. from its pedestal in Bowling Green, and moulded it into Republican bullets.

No doubt his royal majesty of England had read of Narcissus being changed into a flower, Daphne into a laurel, and the teeth of the Dragon springing into armed men; but, probably, he never thought that it was reserved for the quiet and honest burghers of New York city, upon a little island, purchased for $24,*

---

* Hoogh moghende Heeren :
    Hiere is ghister 't schip " Wapen van Amsterdam" aengekomen en is den 23 September uyt Niew Nederland gesijll uyt de rivier Mauritius. Rapporteren dat ons volk daer goed is en vreedigh leven, hare vrouwen hebben oock kinde-

on the outskirts of civilization, to outdo classic mythology by converting this statue of the King of England into a circulating medium of grape and cannister specie, bearing the date of the glorious issue, July the 4th, 1776. So much for the spirit and persistency of the first Dutch settlers and their worthy descendants. But we would be doing evident injustice to the laborious researches of the veracious Mr. Diedrich Knickerbocker if we passed over in silence

---

ren aldaer gebiert; hebben 't eylandt Manhattan van de Wilde gekocht voor de waerde van 60 guildens; is groot 11000 morgen. Hebben daer alle koren half Meij gezayd en half Augustus gemayd. Daervan seyn de monsterkens van Zomerkoren, als tarwe, rogge, garst, haver, boucweyt, kanarigarst, boontjes en vlas.   P. SCHAGHEN.
Amsterdam, 5 Nov. 1626.
[TRANSLATION.]
High and Mighty Lords:
Yesterday arrived the ship "The Arms of Amsterdam." She sailed from the river Mauritias (Hudson), in the New Netherlands, on the 23d September. They report that our folk there are prosperous and live in peace. They have purchased from the Indians, for the sum of 60 guilders, [about $24,] the island Manhattan, which is 11,000 morgen [13,920 acres] large. They have already sowed grain by the middle May, and reapt by the middle of August ; samples of Summer crops have come, such as wheat, rye, barley, oats, buckwheat, Canary seed, beans, and flax.   P. SCHAGHEN.
Amsterdam, 5th Nov., 1626.

the golden age of Walter the Doubter, who ruled from 1633 to 1638. In the charming and graphic style of this truthful historian, whose quiet humor we always read with renewed pleasure, this renowned governor was "descended from a long line of Dutch Burgomasters, who had comported themselves with such singular wisdom and propriety that they were never either heard or talked of, which, next to being universally applauded, should be the ambition of all magistrates. He was a man shut up within himself like an oyster, but then it was allowed he *seldom* said a foolish thing. So incredible was his gravity that he was never known to laugh or to smile through the whole course of a long and prosperous life; and if a joke was uttered in his presence, that set light-minded hearers in a roar, it was observed to throw him into a state of perplexity. He daily took his four stated meals, appropriating exactly an hour to each. His face, that infallible index of the mind, presented a vast expanse unfurrowed by any of those lines and angles which disfigure the human countenance with what is termed expression. He was exactly five feet six inches in height, and six feet five inches in circumference." Such was the renowned Walter the Doubter, and no wonder, in the administration of such a man, " the profoundest tranquility and repose reigned throughout the province." " These were the honest days," continues our historian, " when a passion for cleanliness was the leading principle in domestic economy, when the whole house was constantly in a state of inundation under the discipline of mops, brooms and scrubbing brushes, when every woman also wore pockets—ay, and that, too, of a goodly size, fashioned with patch-work with many curious devices, and ostentatiously worn on the outside. These were, in fact, convenient

receptacles where all good housewives carefully
stored away such things as they wished to have
at hand, by which means they often came to be
incredibly crammed ; and there was a story cur-
rent that the lady of the worthy governor once
had occasion to empty her right pocket in
search of a wooden ladle, when the contents
filled a couple of corn-baskets, and the utensil
was discovered lying among some rubbish in
one corner; but we must not give too much
faith to all these stories—the anecdotes of these
remote periods being very subject to exaggera-
tion." It was also a favorite expression with
our historian, when seated by the fireside of the
old burghers, in some of his various wanderings
from the good old town of Schaghticoke to his
much loved isle of Manahatta, that " We live
in the midst of history, mystery and romance.
He who would find these elements, however,
must not seek for them among the modern im-

provements. He must dig for them as for Kidd the pirate's treasures, in out of the way places, and among the ruins of the past." So we have only to visit these gable-roofed houses, with low, broad chimneys, scattered through our valleys, to learn the history of these good old days. In some of these we hear again

> The humming of the wheel,
>   Strange music of the days gone by,
> We hear the clicking of the reel,
>   Once more we see the spindle fly.

And we well remember how, in our childhood,

> We wondered at the thread
>   That *narrowed* from the snowy wool,
> Much more to see the pieces wed
>   And wind upon the whirling spool.

And we imagine that some of those gathered here have found, by these wide kitchen fireplaces, hearts *all their own*, true and unchanging as the old seven-day clocks brought from the father-land—household treasures more valuable than those of the pirate Kidd, though those supposed treasures were "of gold, yea, of fine gold," for

"The only amaranthine flower on earth
Is *Virtue*—the only lasting treasure, *Truth*."

We all have visited these old hearthstones; to some of us they are a part of our very childhood. Every vein in the marble; every broken corner; every crumbling brick, find their proper places, as we revisit, in memory, the dearest of all familiar spots, for the most vivid pictures of our early lives will always be seen in the light of those hearthstone fires. It is not the glare of noonday that shows the picture best. The sunlight of the Present is often too bright to view the Past: but the *softened* light of those long-ago firesides gives distinctness to the features and character of every loved one, until the invisible world seems to give back, for the time, the forms, and even the voices, of those who have gone before us. Here is the true poetry of social life—and, alas ! the burial-place of our early romance. No wonder, then, that these firesides cause

"A thousand pleasing fantasies
To throng into our memory,"

when so much we loved was gathered here ! No wonder, when the hearth is growing cold, and stranger-hands take away all that is familiar, that we take an ember from the fires that crackled in our childhood, to light up in our hearts that vestal altar which goes out only with our lives.   There is no ruin more sad than a broken and deserted fire-place !   And we have these ruins scattered all through our valley. No ivied tower or broken battlement presents half the look of desertion.   And we never felt this so forcibly as when we visited, in the county of Columbia, on an island in a beautiful lake

about midway between the Catskills and the
Berkshire Hills, an old mansion rapidly falling
into decay—once the property of a distinguished
family, to which a large tract along the Hudson
was ceded by a grant from Queen Anne. At
present but little more than the walls remain,
weather-stained and windowless ; and here,
deeply set in these massive walls, can still be
seen the old fire-places of a century ago. And
here, as we sat musing, while the long twilight
deepened into night, the fire seemed again to
burn upon the hearthstone, perhaps brighter
than it ever did in reality, bathing in rosy light
even the old paintings our fancy hung upon
the walls. And looking into the strange faces
which silently gathered here, we endeavored to
dream out the unwritten histories of a hundred
lives. Here, in these very halls, long, long ago,
were recounted stories of the Revolution, by
those just from the deadly conflict. Here, the

last farewell given by trembling lips, to be dreamed over again and again at Valley Forge, and inciting to courage on the bloody fields of Monmouth—for voices all about us whispered deeds of truth and daring; and in the gloom of the old ruins gathered that noble family, whose name and deeds are a part of our history!

And here, a short time ago, it is said that above one of these old mantles there was found a quaint POEM, commemorating an incident of the Revolution. It was written upon some legal cap paper, moulded and blurred by time. Whether some youthful Chatterton in this way attempted to deceive the people, we will allow antiquarians and the curious to decide. This strange poem, in half-forgotten English characters, was dedicated to the Children in the Forests—more frequently known as "The Babes in the Woods." And in a trembling hand, which

is in itself suspicious, was written the following
queer and ungrammatical couplet :

> "*One of the many Poems 'wrote'*
>
> BY
>
> *The talkative female*—ANNIE K. DOTE."

POEM.

"THE CAPTAIN WHO TOOK THE DISTRICT SCHOOL"

All day long the snow clouds rolled
Up from the mountains, fold on fold;
All day long in a gloomy veil
The sky was lost and the sun was pale :
Along the Berkshires, bleak and gray,
The storm-king muttering seemed to say,
" Day mingle with Night, Night mingle with
  Day."
Mingling of Spirits truly *black* and *gray*,
Gray day, black night, Spirits far more real
Than old Macbeth's witches " in the land o' the
  Leal."

Happy, indeed, were the circles that night
Unbroken around the firesides bright!
But in many a window a beacon shone
Casting its light through the ghostly storm,
Telling of hearts and of firesides warm
Waiting the coming of some one gone.
"What made sister go, my mother dear,
For the night is cold and the fire-side's bright?"
The mother says, with a falling tear,
"My daughter, you know 'tis Sunday night:
And since the days when I was young,
With lips as sweet as sister's are—
I *mean*, to sing the songs then sung
Through all this section near and far—
This night was set apart for those,
Who had a suit of Sunday clothes,
Who loved, and *sometimes* dared propose.
Sometimes at home, sometimes away,
And sometimes e'en till morning gray,
We sailed upon the moonlit lake

Watching the stars and 'aerolites'
Throughout those summer Sunday nights,
Unwilling for the spell to break :
But never in a night so wild
Was I from home, my darling child.
And these were days long, long ago,
Days which for years you can not know,
Too soon to come, too soon to go.
And strange it is that one so young
Should hang upon my foolish tongue;
Strange that the same 'old story' still
Should please our children just as well.—
But I wonder why they do not come."
And the mother peers into the gloom;
But naught is seen save the whirling snow,
And she turns again to the fireside glow.
"Such a storm, my child, I never knew,
And childhood I passed among hills and dales
That caught the roughest, wildest gales
That ever swept a valley through;

But such a night, so bleak and wild,
I never knew before, my child;
And yet in memory I hold
A story, by my grand-sire told,
And I'll repeat the silly rhyme
To pass away the idle time :

" There was a Captain, free and bold,
As ancient chroniclers have told,
Who, fighting in our fathers' cause
For freedom's right and freedom's laws,
Found time, at least upon his sword,
To write a name his soul adored,
And build huge castles in the air
All furnished for his darling fair.
Would that such castles were more real !
How soon at Beauty's shrine we'd kneel
And make an eloquent appeal
To hearts like gun-boats clad in steel !
    But, to return unto our story :

Our hero, from the fields of glory,

With battle-scars (upon his clothes),

On horse-back, through the drifting snows

Was struggling toward a beacon-light

Just glimmering through that dreadful night.

Alas ! fair maid with fluttering heart,

Your hopes no aid can now impart,

For, floundering coolly in a bank,

The exhausted steed and rider sank.

The whirling snow and blinding sleet

Would soon have made his winding sheet :

But thanks ! there was a School House near,

   And hope began to swell his breast,

   For there, he thought, he might have rest

From such a night so wild and drear.

The deed was suited to the thought—

   The Horseman struggled through the snow,

   The door was forced with a sturdy blow

And in the gallant steed was brought.

The tinder-box a fire supplied
Which, roaring up the chimney wide,
Imparted cheer to the cozy room
Which else had seemed a living tomb,
Wrapped in the midnight and the gloom.
The horse, thawed out, began to paw,
Asking for oats and accustomed straw,
Unmindful that he had the quarters
Where farmers sent their sons and daughters.
The Captain quietly looked around
On well-worn books and well-cut seats,
Adorned with countless 'Bills' and 'Petes,'
And fell, at last, in slumber sound :   •
To dream—of whom we must not tell :
You guess, and 'twill be just as well.

Suffice to say, in about a day,
For the simple fee of an X or a V
He answered 'yes' to questions three :
That is, 'Love,' 'Honor,' and 'Obey,'—
They've changed the form some now-a-day—

Then hired a sleigh and felt O. K.

But he never forgot, nor his darling 'Jule,'
The night he took the District School !"*

So much for the written and the unwritten language of the old hearthstones of Columbia. Nor can we look at the tiles brought from Holland, quaintly illustrating familiar passages

---

* As real poetry generally needs an explanatory note, we feel constrained to say, for the benefit of *logical* readers :

There's truth in rhyme as well as prose,
It's only *dressed* in different clothes ;
Yet many critics, by the way,
Make light of poetry, and say
It's *flimsy* stuff, and very thin
To robe such things as nature in ;
And blush for Beauty when they see
Her form in such loose drapery.
'Tis true some charms should be arrayed
In thicker stuff than 's sometimes made ;
But, ever since our earliest youth,
We 've often heard of "naked truth,"
And as the thinnest gauze or lace
Better reveals the beauteous face
Than thicker stuff ; this, then, forsooth,
More nearly shows the naked truth ;
And hence the reason why some choose
This flimsy rhyme instead of prose,
Thinner instead of thicker clothes.

in Bible history, without thinking how happy
were these fireside gatherings compared with
the modern feasts of pampered luxury. How
the old Legends and Traditions come thronging
upon us mingled with recollections of fireside
laughter and fireside tears! Here the story of
the " Storm Ship" was repeated over and over
again, until we knew it as well as the story of
Blue Beard and the ill-fated Fatima; and as it
is peculiarly 'and distinctively *the* legend of
the early settlers, we must not pass it over
in silence. And still, about the glowing fire-
places of olden dwellings scattered along our
River, it is repeated in the long winter even-
ings somewhat as follows :

" The word, one day, was given from the fort,
standing on the spot now known as the Bat-
tery, that a ship was coming up the bay. It
passed from mouth to mouth, and street to
street, and soon put the little town of New

Amsterdam into a bustle. We can easily imagine the arrival of a ship in those early times
of the settlement was an event of no small im-
portance to the inhabitants. The artist waited
for his tools, the burgomaster for his supply of
Hollands, the good vrow for her gown and the
little children," who, according to tradition—by
way of parenthesis—did not look half as much
like olive plants as large plump cabbages, "were
continually in want of pocket handkerchiefs,
and stuff for aprons. It was, in short, the great
yearly event of the Town, and from one end of
the year to the other, 'the ship,' 'the ship,' was
the continual conversation." Many were, there-
fore, assembled upon the wharfs. Knots of old
weather-beaten sailors, and crowds of the Mr.
and Mrs. Burghers, all philosophically conjec-
turing what could be its mission. "On she
bore, steadily up the bay, and although repeat-
edly hailed, made no reply, but, sailing against

both wind and tide, passed up the Hudson.

"Week after week, and month after month elapsed, but she never returned; and it was related that over the wide waters of Haverstraw and Tappan Zee, she could be seen careening when night and storm wrapped the river in gloom, and in the midst of the turmoil you could hear the Captain giving orders in good Low Dutch. Some suggested that if it really was a supernatural apparition, as there was every reason to believe, it might be Hendrick Hudson and his crew of the 'Half Moon,' who, it was well known, had once run aground in the upper part of the river, in seeking a Northwest passage to China." And perhaps it was the shadowy crew returning to their periodical revels in the mountains, for it was generally reported that Hendrick Hudson and his men really haunted the Catskills, and these are supposed to have been the ghostly nine-pin players, who some time afterward entertained old Rip Van Winkle so kindly, and left him in sweet repose, apart from his family cares,

" To sleep through years of mighty wars,
And wake to science grown to more."
To find the sign of *another George;*
Swinging above the Tavern door."

People who live in this vicinity, still insist that they occasionally see her under some steep bluff of the Highlands, all in deep shadow excepting her top-sails glittering in the moonlight.

" See you beneath yon cloud so dark,
Fast gliding along a gloomy bark;
Her sails are full, tho' the wind is still,
And there blows not a breath, her sails to fill.

    *   *   *   *   *

By skeleton shapes her sails are furled,
And the hand that steers is not of this world."

And why hasn't our river as good right to a Phantom Ship as Cape Horn, New Haven Harbor or Deadman's Isle in the Gulf of St. Lawrence!

Another of these marvelous legends, long ago, in some idle moments was put into verse. We would not vouch for its truthfulness, and the nearer we get to the locality of the scene, we are sorry to say, the less it is believed, and yet the account was told us in our childhood for very truth.

On the banks of the Hudson near old Dobbs'
    Ferry,
A mansion still stands deserted and dreary
Around whose gables the ivy creeps,
Around whose walls even silence sleeps.
Deserted and drear is the ruined place
As it were the grave of a buried race.
Tradition says that long ago—
Perhaps a hundred years or so—
A family came from a town somewhere,
With obvious intentions of settling there;
For a mansion they built prodigious in size
Which filled the neighbors with such sur-
    prise

That it literally made them stick out their
    eyes.
(Pardon the muse for being precise,
You, I mean, who are overnice;
You who think the sacred nine
Breathe inspiration all divine,
And never stoop to earthly things,
But always soar on heavenly wings.)
And as the right is with the strong,
No way had they to redress the wrong;
But, strange to say, on a certain day,
A woman in white on the grounds appeared—
Perhaps a fairy, perhaps a fay—
And marshalled them all and led them away;
For all who looked upon her feared,
And trembling could not but obey;
And so, deserted were those halls.
For none returned who once were seen,
And very few were those I ween
Who dared to pass those mansion walls;
And many the legends, mysterious and queer,
About that home of perpetual fear.
'Twas said that often at midnight hour,
When the moon was full, on the chimney
    tower
Her cold light trembled with fitful glare,

And music strange filled earth and air,
As 'twere a dirge for the freed from pain,
Or sorrow subdued for those that remain—
Sorrow! of all life's song the refrain!

But, to be brief, the strangest of all these stories was that, on a certain evening in the vicinity of the Highlands, a wedding was taking place in good old style between a Mr. Hendrick and a Miss Katrina, and just as the "you do" and the "I will" had made the two a unit, a fairy dressed in white came into the room and took away the lovely and interesting Katrina. Hendrick and the respective families for a number of days spent most of the time in weeping, until it was reported that, in the vicinity of the deserted mansion, *two* were seen, and both were dressed like fairies. Hendrick immediately left for this locality, examines the old deserted halls by moonlight, but finds nothing of his Katrina. Overcome with grief and disappointment he

seats himself upon the door-step and sadly
hums the following measure:

It is sweet to sit at evening,
When the west is painted red,
And to think of friends once with us,
Of the living and the dead.
It is sweet to hear at midnight,
Music stealing through the air,
While we feel our spirits rising
Heavenward on that silver stair:
Ever fonder, ever dearer,
Seems our youth that hastened by,
And we love to live in memory,
When our fond hopes fade and die.
Yes! like forests that seem fairer,
When the leaves their freshness lose,
So the past those leaves now fading,
Tinged with memory lovelier grows.
The echoes startled from their sleep
Had hardly died away,
When forth from out the shadows deep
The fairy held her way;
No shadow she threw in the moon's pale
    beams,
But, like a passing form of light,
Presented herself to our hero's sight—

Quite lost in sorrow and his dreams—
And thus the fairy begun to say:
I've watched you, Hendrick, for many a day,
Weeping and wailing, but all in vain,
For ne'er can you see your darling again.
Weep for Katrina with eyes so blue;
Weep! well you may, for she was treu—
Few maidens ever loved as she—
Weep! Weep! it doesn't trouble me;
But 'though I'm not moved by pity,
I admire you for your courage;
And, if you can guess a riddle,
I will make you, too, immortal,
So that you can live forever
With your darling, your Katrina.
Where grows the flower, and what's its name,
Which blooms in winter and summer the
        same,
The language of which some say is true,
Some say is false, now what say you?

Our hero knew not what to say
In answer to the cruel fay;
But a muse, from a bright and distant sphere,
Swiftly to his rescue flew,
And, breathing softly in his ear,

Whispered the *answer* plain and clear;
And to the fairy, mute with surprise,
He answered, somewhat in this wise:

Say not all the flowers of the valley fade,
When pa nted leaves on the ground are laid,
And the carpet of nature, curiously dyed,
Covers the vale and the mountain side;
Oh! no; there's a flower *earth's frost* never nips
In many a valley—the sweet *two-lips*
We find them in bowers of nature wild
Wherever we see the forest child,
Where'er streamlets flow or soft winds blow,
In lands that are wrapped in eternal snow,
We find these flowers, for sun or shade
Ne'er blights nor blasts nor makes them fade;
And even more than this is true,
For when *they're pressed* they bloom anew.
The fairy vanished but again appeared
Leading Katrina through the ruined halls,
And in the silence of that midnight hour,
Again were joined those hands once rudely
    torn.
We leave the hearer here to guess the rest,
How many times "two-lips" were fondly
    pressed;

4

How long they sat and watched the moon-
    light fall
Upon the gable-roofs and ivied wall.
And still some people of that section say,
That when the stars roll in their middle way,
The immortal pair amid the ruins stand,
Just as they should be *always, hand in hand.*

A Swedish traveler, moreover, tells us that
the early settlers of our towns and villages had
seats on the stoops of their dwellings, which, in
the evening, were filled with young people, and
passers by were obliged to greet everybody un-
less they would shock the politeness of the people. In these good old days when, according to
Irving, the heart of a lover could not contain
more than one lady at a time, for quite evident
reasons, we recognize a blissful ignorance of the
" Blue Laws of Connecticut," for it has never
along our river been considered a crime for a
person to repeat the " House that Jack Built"
because therein the gentlemen

    " All tattered and torn
Kissed the maiden all forlorn."

But how far the politeness of our mothers can be traced in some of our modern bellisms, we can only refer again to the language of Mr. Knickerbocker: "Ah! blissful and never-to-be-forgotten age, when there were neither public commotions nor private quarrels, neither persecutions nor trials nor punishments; when the shad in the river were all salmon; when every man attended to what little business he was lucky enough to have, or neglected it if he pleased without asking the opinion of his neighbor; when nobody meddled with concerns above his comprehension, or neglected to correct his own conduct in his zeal to pull to pieces the characters of others." These were, indeed, good old days when the renowned Wouter Van Twiller and the fat aldermen of the quiet city of New Amsterdam ruled in peace and tranquility with-

out issuing twenty-four paged proclamations;
when the good old burghers never disturbed
themselves to see whether the gates of Janus
were shut or open, but quietly imbibed rich
draughts of inspiration like the ancient poets
through *oaten* straws, quaffing nectar that
looked very much like old Holland, and eating
Ambrosia that had all the appearance of dough-
nuts. And while we, to-day, rejoice at the
prosperity of this beautiful valley, happy in the
arts and refinements of a rich and later civilization, we still love to wander among the monuments of our early settlers and, it may be, moisten
with our tears the ivy which we ourselves
have planted. Slowly but surely every year re-
moves some landmark of the past. Even the
places where our fathers worshiped, with their
spires pointing to heaven from the very ground
hallowed by their ashes, are passing away; yes

"They all are passing from our land,
   Those churches old and gray,
In which our fathers used to stand,
   In years gone by to pray."

But there is in the *poetry of this river*
something still more interesting to the genius of
our people than even these crumbling ruins or
the strange traditions of the early settlers.
Here the great struggle for freedom has conse-
crated many a spot. The places where our
fathers met for council, the ruined ramparts
they defended with their lives; redoubts and bas-
tions, battered and broken: these are eloquent
to every heart ! Saratoga, Stillwater, Crown
Point, Old Ticonderoga, Stony Point, West
Point, White Plains, the Heights of Harlem
and the Heights of Brooklyn—each has a sep-
arate page in the story of the Revolution! and
to all minds this history is filled with the poetic
element! The character of our generals, the un-

flinching courage of those who with bleeding
feet tracked their way to liberty over the snows
of seven winters ; the sublime heroism and
devotion of a people imperiling everything but
their honor in the strife for their country : all
these afford the noblest material for lofty
song, for the poetic element is defined to be a
spiritual sympathy with whatever is beautiful,
grand or sublime, and over our battlefields and
around " our monuments which lift themselves
toward Heaven as if to tell the angels that here
human blood has flown for human freedom,"
the very air is freighted with the beautiful, the
grand and the sublime, and we feel justified in
our assertion that there is no other place in all
our country where poetry and romance are so
strangely blended with the heroic of our history.

To destroy the communication between
the Eastern and the Southern and Middle
States, was the plan of the English, hence the

Hudson reaching almost from Lake Champlain to the Ocean, and forming, as it were, a natural boundary, was the scene of many struggles; and from the time the first messenger sped along the "Old Post Road," on the way from New York to Albany, spreading the dread news of War, the banks of the Hudson glowed with the beacon lights of liberty, burning brighter and brighter unto the perfect day. In the North, on the plains of Saratoga, we see homeless and wandering families, fleeing from the sound of war. We read the sad story of Jane McRea, blanching the cheek of mother and maiden. We read the long suffering of our northern army, crowned at last by the surrender of Burgoyne. This campaign was frequently referred to in the popular songs of the day. And we have selected a few lines from "The Old Saratoga Song," as a specimen of the early poetry of our Country. .

"The Nineteenth of September,
  The morning cool and clear,
Brave Gates rode through our army,
  Each Soldier's heart to cheer;
'Burgoyne,' he cried, 'advances,
  But we will never fly,
No, rather than surrender,
  We'll fight him 'till we die.'
The news was quickly brought us
  The enemy was near,
And all along our lines, then,
  There was no sign of fear;
It was above Stillwater
  We met, at noon that day,
And every one expected
  To see a bloody fray.
Six hours the battle lasted,
  Each heart was true as gold,
The British fought like Lions,
  And we like Yankees bold;
The leaves with blood were crimson,
  And then brave Gates did cry,
"'Tis diamond now cut diamond,'
  We'll beat them boys, or die ! "

This early minstrelsy of the Revolution **may**

not be eminently poetical, and yet, these songs
and ballads will in the years to come, be prized
far more highly, than many of the popular poems
of to-day. "The altars may have been humble
yet the the fires burned toward Heaven." We
give another valuable and historic specimen of
these poems, which have outlived the papers for
which they were written, and have come to be
regarded American antiquities. It may suggest
the enumeration of ships in the second book
of the Iliad, but its *quaintness* has probably no
parallel in ancient or modern literature.

THE LOSS IN BURGOYNE'S CAMPAIGN.

```
"British Prisoners, by convention,   .   .   2,442
Foreigners, by contra-vention,.  .   .   .  2,198
Tories, sent across the lake,   .   .   .   .  1,100
Burgoyne and his suit in state,   .   .   .      12
Sick and wounded, bruised and pounded, }
Ne'er so much before confounded,   .   }   528
Prisoners of war, before convention,   .    400
Deserters, come with kind intention,   .    300
They lost at Bennington great battle,  }
Where Starke's glorious arms did rattle. }  1,220
```

Killed in September and October,   . .   600
Ta'en by brave Brown, some drunk some
    sober, ...   413
Slain by high-famed Herkerman,   ⎱
On both flanks, both rear and van,   ⎰   300
Indians, suttlers, butchers, drovers,   ⎫
Enough to crowd large plains all over, ⎪
And those whom grim death did prevent ⎪
From fighting 'gainst our continent,   ⎬ 4,413
And also those who stole away,   ⎪
Lest they down their arms should lay, ⎪
Abhorring that obnoxious day.   ⎭
The whole make fourteen thousand men, ⎱
· Who may not with us fight again."   ⎰   14,000

But the great central place was West Point, perched like an eagle's nest among the high-lands and completely commanding the river. The English at once recognized this as the Gibraltar of the Hudson, and attempted to buy for gold this strong-hold of the colonists. But even treachery was unable to avail any-thing, except to erect a monument of infamy to tell the fate of those who are Arnolds to their country. This darkest plot, nursed in so much secrecy, was, in the morning, preached upon the house-tops. Andre was taken and a monument erected to the memory of Paulding, for there were not *then* two Arnolds in our country; not two who could be bought by British gold. "No!" said Paulding, "if you would give us ten thousand guineas you would not stir one step."

Andre, who has sometimes seemed the second Sydney of England, young, brave and accomplished, was condemned as a spy and executed; and we may be pardoned while speaking of the execution of Andre in referring to the case of Nathan Hale, "perhaps the best educated young man in our country, who had left the halls of Yale University to die, if necessary, for liberty. In attempting to return to the American lines he was seized and brought before Sir William Howe, who ordered him to be executed the next morning, and the sentence was carried

into effect in the most barbarous manner. He
asked if he might see a friend, one he loved better than all things but liberty, one who had
given him up to his country, and he was de-
nied. He asked for a Bible and it was refused;
even his last request that a clergyman might
visit him was rejected with *oaths*. What a
striking contrast to the conduct of Washington,
who signed Andre's death-warrant with tears;
and, more cruel than all this, Hale's letters,
written the night before his death to his be-
trothed, his mother and other dear friends, were
broken open and burned in order that the
Rebels should not know that they had a man in
their army who could die with so much firm-
ness. We have also read that "she who would
have been his bride went with her father at
night through the British lines, took his body
from the gibbet and carried it to their own
home!" Can the English historian find nothing

in this to extenuate the fate of Andre, and would not England, to-day, erect a monument to the memory of Paulding rather than to the memory of Arnold? West Point seems, moreover, the connecting link between the history of the past and the present. The great names that must ever live in our country's story; the wildness of the cliffs, the beauty and sublimity which are blended here; everything speaks of freedom.

"The rocks, the rills, the woods and templed hills," nature's instructors, *all*, raise their voices in chanting the glory of those whose deeds can never die. Here, too, are gathered historic relics as if met in centennial gathering, eloquent trophies of victory; broken artillery of the field of Saratoga which "fought a good fight and kept the faith," and the old flags bearing the red cross of England telling the glory and shame of our Mother Country. Fitting place

4

to muse upon our history, and as we once stood
under the monument of "Kosciusko, sur-
rounded on every side by ever-varying beauty—
the Mattewan mountains of the Indians—we
thought of the bold charge of the young
Polish hero at the battle of Bemis Heights; his
night interview with Lafayette, and after our
country had taken its place among the nations
of the world, his sad fate upon the field of War-
saw, where the liberty of Poland died with
Kosciusko. And there, under that monument
erected to his memory, we felt, as we have never
felt before, how "sublime a thing a free people
is." Autumn had touched with bright tints
the leaves of the forest, and every bush and
shrub, glowing with the rich hectic of a dying
year, seemed to say, like the burning bush of
Midian : "Take thy shoes from off thy feet for
the place on which thou standest is holy
ground." And, over all, the rich sunset sprink-

ling its rosy flowers over the summit of the
cliffs, or rather a hanging sea of golden cyclades
—a dream of the poets, half of earth and half
of heaven.

" What 'though no cloister gray or ivied column
    Along this cliff their sombre ruins rear;
What 'though no frowning tower or temple
        solemn
Of despots tell and superstition here,
Yet sights and sounds, at which the world
        have wondered,
Within these wild ravines have had their birth;
    Young freedom's cannons from these glens
        have thundered,
    And sent their startling echoes o'er the
        the earth;
And not a verdant glade or mountain hoary
    But treasures up within the glorious story."

And while we mused upon the history of this
river lying at our feet, with its points of interest crowding each other and almost blending,
we thought, as in the mediæval days, there
were little shrines and chapels scattered along

the route to the Holy Land, where weary pil-
grims might turn aside from their journey to
pray; so along the banks of the Hudson, from
the "Wilderness to the sea," are scattered
shrines for patriotic devotion, where a whole
people, coming up from the red sea of war and
journeying—God grant—to the bright land of
promise, may bow in sincerity and thankfulness!
And, also, as in our art galleries we sometimes
turn away from the battle-scenes—although
they tell of victory and glory—and find relief
and pleasure in some little household picture,
so there are little stories, and some of them
embalmed in poetry, which will live as long as
"The Banks and Braes o' Bonnie Doon." For
we imagine the leaves will never fade nor fall
from that "old familiar tree" a little ways from
the City of New York, and immortalized by
that beautiful lyric, which every child knows by
heart, by the poet who wrote "My Mother's

Bible,"—"Woodman, spare that Tree." And where in our language is there a more beautiful picture !

> "When but an idle boy
>   I sought its grateful shade.
> In all their gushing joy,
>   Here too my sisters played,
> My mother kissed me here,
>   My father pressed my hand,
> Forgive the foolish tear,
>   But let the old oak stand."

On one occasion, when Mr. Russel was singing it at Boulogne, an old gentleman in the audience, moved by the simple and touching beauty of the lines, rose and said : I beg your pardon, but was the tree really spared !" " It was," answered Mr. Russel, and the old gentleman resumed his seat amid the enthusiastic plaudits of the whole assembly. Truly

> " Its glory and renown
>   Are spread o'er land and sea."

And a little to the north, we have " Sleepy Hollow," with its murmuring brook, rendered famous for the ride of the "Headless Horseman," the woes and mishaps of Ichabod Crane, the unsuccessful schoolmaster, and the blooming Katrina Van Tassel; and still further to the north,

" The moon looks down on an old Cro-nest,
She mellows the shade on his shaggy breast."

And we take a trip with the culprit Fay,
    In his lovely boat of shining shell ;
'Till above the Highlands far away,
    The Catskills blue from the valley swell,
And leaving the boat on the silvery strand,
    We take a seat in the charmed car,
And over the fair and moonlit land,
    We pass like the light of a falling star.

Right over the " Man in the Mountains, who, for six thousand years, has ever looked up at the changing beauty of the sky,

" Counting the stars in the bright jeweled
    crown
As they roll so silently o'er,

With their golden wheels which leave not
    a trace
Upon God's azure floor.

And, as the moonlight bathes his upturned
brow, we imagine, like another Endymion re-
clining on the bank, he is beloved by

      " That bright-eyed Goddess
      Whom mortals call the moon."

And a voice, soft, gentle and low, whispers in
his ear : "Remember, Endymion of the Mountain, the doom of the culprit Fay, for although
Diana presses thy cheek whenever she sinks to
rest, beware, it is only moonshine !" And now
a drowsy murmur rises in the still night air,
as it were borne upward on floating chariots of
spray,

  " From greens and shades where the
      Catterskill leaps
From cliffs where the wood flowers cling,"

and we recall the legend and the lines of Bry-

ant, which express so beautifully the well-nigh
fatal dream

> " Of that dreaming one
> By the base of that icy steep
> When over his stiffening limbs begun
> The deadly slumbers of frost to creep.
> *   *   *   *
> There pass the chasers of seal and whale,
> With their weapons quaint and grim,
> And bands of warriors in glittering mail,
> And herdsmen and hunters huge of limb,
> There are naked arms with bow and spear,
> And furry gauntlets the carbine rear.
> There are mothers—and Oh, how sadly their
> eyes
> On their children's white brows rest !
> There are youthful lovers—the maiden lies
> In a seeming sleep on the chosen breast,
> There are fair, wan women with moon-struck
> air,
> The snow-stars flecking their long, loose
> hair."

The dashing water is again lost far away in
the deep forest, and we stand in the pale light
of morning upon the cliff in front of the Moun-

tain House, to take in at a glance the wide
beauty of our River. Night is fast melting in the
dawn, a deep blue rests upon the whole valley
as it were a sea lying silent at our feet, and the
Berkshire Hills seem like immense waves roll-
ing on from the distant horizon. Patiently we
wait the Sun's advent, and as the rosy dawn
announces the morning coming with " looks all
vernal and with cheeks all bloom," the *windows*
of the Mountain House one after another be-
gins to reveal undreamed visions of loveliness,
and unmindful of the words of the culprit Fay,
it were really difficult to tell which had the
deeper interest, the Sun's rising in the East, or
the daughters in the West. The rosy clouds of
the one; the tender blushes of the other ; the
opening eye-lids of the morning, or the opening
eye-lids of innocence, the bright ambrosial
locks hanging far and wide along the deep blue
chiseled mountain side, or the *uncombed* rip-

ples which, like mountain streams receiving additions from other sources, would probally become beautiful water-falls.   In four minutes more by solar time, and the sun would sprinkle the golden dust of light over the valley of the Hudson.   The East is all aglow, and, *as we stand musing the fire burns*, yes brighter and brighter, as if the distant hills were an altar, and a sacrifice was being offered up to the God of Day.

> "And see! The sun himself on wings
> Of glory up the East he springs,
> Angel of light which from the time
> Those Heavens began their march sub-
>   .lime,
> Has first of all the starry choir
> Trod in his maker's steps of fire."

And as merry voices ring out from the window frames of Beauty, we can but add, to complete the sketch—

And see! The daughters in the West
In mirthful glee and half—*suppressed*,
Angels of morn! who, from the time
Man ever saved a single dime,
Have always longed and prayed to go
Wherever there was *any* show.

Cities and villages below us spring into being, and misty shapes rise from the valley, as
if Day had rolled back the stone from the
Sepulchre of Night, and it was rising trans-
figured to Heaven. Adown and up the river
for the distance of sixty miles, sails of sloops
and schooners drift lazily along, while below
us the little

"ferry boats plie
Like slow shuttles through the sunny warp
Of threaded silver from a thousand brooks."

Truly the Catskills were a fitting place for
the artist Cole to gather inspiration to complete that beautiful series of engravings "The

Voyage of Life," for no finer mountains in all
the world overlook a finer river.

And if the groves were sacred to the ancients
where the *fabled* Orpheus sung, sacred indeed
to us must be the River of Sunnyside, Idle-
wild and Undercliff, the home of Irving, of
Willis and Morris! all of whom but a short
time ago laid down the pen which wrote the
heart's own language, and made our Hudson
the Rhine of America. Nor can we speak the
name of Washington Irving, without thinking
of that monument more lasting than brass,
which he has erected to his memory whose
foundation lies deep in the hearts of the American people. For as the lovely vales of the
Arno are always associated with the name of
Virgil, and the beautiful banks of Ayr are immortal as the name of Burns, so the name of
Irving will always be associated with the name
of the Hudson. In his own words "It has

been my lot in the course of a somewhat wandering life to behold some of the streams of the
old world, most renowned in history and song;
yet none have been able to efface the pictures
of my native stream, stamped early on my
mind;" and again he says: "I thank God that
I was born on the banks of the Hudson, for I.
fancy I can trace much of what is good and
pleasant in my own heterogeneous compound to
my early companionship with this glorious
river." How the literature of our country and
particularly our river is indebted to his genius!

And we ought not to forget how the sublime
and beautiful in nature are interwoven with the
political and moral development of a people.
We can not live in the midst of this beautiful
scenery, without feeling its inspiration in our
hearts, inciting us to something nobler and better. It is impossible to be slaves where all nature speaks of liberty; and in tracing the prog-

ress of freedom from the time when the words
of Luther electrified Europe, we see its first
footsteps, like the *approach of morning* upon
the mountains, and along the banks of rivers!
We see the lights of religious liberty, blazing
upon the clear streams of Switzerland; we hear
the voice of Calvin from mountain-walled Ge-
neva ; and when almost exiled from Europe,
takes up the words of Knox, "Give me Scot-
land or I die ; " and in the deep fastnesses of
her hills, and in the deeper hearts of a people
who drank in liberty with the very air they
breathed, awaited patiently the hour of proclaiming to the world the right of private judg-
ment, both in religion and in politics ; ever
teaching that noble sentiment of *loyalty to con-
viction*, which led Charles the first through the
windows of Whitehall upon the scaffold, and
banished the House of Stuart from the Throne
of England. It crosses the ocean and lays here

the foundation of a Republic, where civil and religious *government* becomes civil and religious *liberty*, and the Divine Right of Kings becomes the *Divine Rights of Men.* And here along our fair streams this transplanted liberty will ever flourish, and along this the fairest stream it will gather Poetry from its Legends, Hope from its History, and a Consciousness of God from its Beauty.

APPENDIX.

Many of the names of the towns and cities along the Hudson at once suggest their origin. We give the derivation and signification of some of the most important.

Brooklyn—*Breukelen*, Broken-land, from the unevenness of the surrounding country.

The old Dutch name of Westchester was *Vreedlandt*, Peace-land.

Haverstraw, some say a "place of straw;" others, "out of straw."

Stony Point retains its Dutch name, translated.

The Donder Bergh and the Kills of Jans Peek retain their Dutch names. The promontory just above, called Antonies Neus, corrupted

into St. Anthony's Nose, was named after An-
tony de Hooge, Secretary of the Colony of Rensselaerwyck.

Newburgh, settled by the Palatines, signifying *New Town.*

Yonkers, *Yonk-herr*, named after the young
lord or *young sir* of the Phillipsie manor.

Sing Sing, called from the Chinese city *Tsing
Tsing*, a name given to the place by a merchant
who traded with China.

Poughkeepsie, Indian name *Apokeepsing*, signifying "Safe Harbor."

Wilt-wick, the old Dutch name for the town
of Kingston, literally Wild wick or Indian wick.

The Dutch built a Redoubt on the banks of
the creek, where it flows into the river. The
kill took the name of Redoubt kill, afterwards
Rundout, hence *Rondout.*

Hyde Park, named in honor of Lady Ann
Hyde, afterwards Queen of England.

Rhinebeck ; some say, a combination of two
words, Beekman and Rhine, a family from the
Rhine who first settled there. Perhaps the better

derivation is the resemblance of the cliffs to those on the middle Rhine, *Beck*, in Dutch, signifying cliff.

Hudson is supposed to be the point where Hendrick Hudson anchored, the 16th of September, 1609, and sent little boats up the river.

Claverack, *Het Clauver Rack*, "the Clover reach." The reach at Hudson is one of the thirteen reaches into which the river is divided.

Kinderhook, signifying "Children's corner."

Stuyvesant, named after old Peter Stuyvesant.

Coeymans, named after one of the early inhabitants. The creek and neighborhood originally were called Hockatock.

Castleton, named from Castle Island, where the Dutch had a fort.

Po-can-ti-ko was the old Indian name for Tarrytown.

Coxsackie and Nyack are both of Indian origin.

Greenbush, Het Greene-Bosch, the Dutch name for "The Pine Woods."

Albany, once called Bever-wyck, and Williamstadt. A fort was erected there in 1623, and the place was sometimes called Fort Aurania. Its present name was given in honor of the Duke of Albany in 1664, on the surrender of the fort to the English. The Indians called it Shaunaugh-ta-da, or once "The Pine Plains."

Troy in 1786 called Ferryhook. In 1787 called Rensselaerwyck. In the fall of 1787 the settlers began to use the name of Vanderheyden, who once owned a great part of the ground where the city now stands. Jan. 9th, 1789, the Freeholders of the town met and gave it the name of Troy.

The river was called for the first few years after its discovery, by some of the settlers, the "Manhattes," after a tribe of Indians living at its mouth, by others the "Mauritius" and "de groote" River, (The great river,) afterwards called the North river, not so much from its course as to distinguish it from the Delaware, which they called the "South" river. The In-

dians called it the "Shate-muc." The English
gave it the name of The Hudson River, by way
of continual claim as Hendrick Hudson was of
English birth. The Spaniards called it "The
River of the Mountains."

www.ingramcontent.com/pod-product-compliance
Lightning Source LLC
Chambersburg PA
CBHW020042030726
47499CB00007B/2543